THE CB RADIO CAPER

A Mystery

by Gary Paulsen

cover by Monroe Eisenberg

SCHOLASTIC INC.
New York Toronto London Auckland Sydney Tokyo

ISBN: 0-590-12081-6

12 11 10 9 8 7 6 5 4 3   4 5 6 7 8/8

Printed in the U.S.A.   01

CONTENTS

CRIMES WITHOUT A CLUE

Malcolm Westerman, known to his friends as Mallard—a nickname that had stuck with him for most of his fourteen years—slipped another piece of gum into his mouth and bit down.

He was thinking, his glasses propped on top of his head, his longish hair pulled back from his face. And when he thought, he turned into a gum-chewing maniac. Sometimes he went through eight or ten pieces if the problem was hairy enough. Usually a full pack of five did the trick.

He was in his room, surrounded by posters and shelves full of books. His folks jokingly called it a disaster area because Mallard didn't keep it all that neat, but it was where he thought best. And right now he had to think better than he'd ever thought before.

In front of him, on a low table he'd made from an old door propped on concrete blocks, lay the latest edition of the newspaper.

"KIDNAPPING RING CONTINUES TO OPERATE," the headline blazed. Then, in smaller type: "Authorities Baffled; Are Investigators Inept?"

The story beneath the headline amounted to little more than a rehash of earlier articles. In splashy phrases it told of the "...four abductions to date"—which was fact. Then the article spent five long paragraphs tearing the local police department apart for not "...protecting the citizens" — which was not fact. The police were doing the best they could with the men they had available. The problem was that the police — and now the FBI — hadn't been notified of the crimes until each was at least 24 hours old. The victims had been too frightened. And since there were no clues of any kind whatsoever — absolutely nothing — there wasn't anything the police could do.

As for the bit about the investigators being inept, that was a lot of hogwash. Mallard's father was David Westerman, chief inspector on the city police department. He was not inept, not in the least, but he *was* mad—not only at the kidnappers but also at the editors and just about everybody else in the world.

He'd even threatened to quit his job, and Mallard couldn't ever remember a case that had put his father on the edge of quitting. But then he'd never seen a case that caused the police commissioner to call every night either — just to ask if there were any new leads since quitting time.

Mallard took another piece of gum out of his pocket, peeled the paper off, and bit down. Was that five pieces or six? He tried to remember, couldn't, decided it didn't matter, and leaned back on his studio couch.

Ever since he was a little kid, Mallard's dad had talked to him about the way crimes were solved. He had explained how important even the smallest clue could be. A remark someone made carelessly, an article that was somehow out of place—anything unusual—might have some bearing on a case. And Inspector Westerman had always emphasized the importance of thinking, sort of meditating, about all sides of the case he was working on. A good detective doesn't just run around looking for clues. He figures out what those clues might mean.

Malcolm thought his dad was just about the

best detective who ever solved a crime, and he wanted to be just like him. Of course, he couldn't go around and visit the scene of the crime along with the police and the reporters, but he figured there was nothing to keep him from helping his dad on the side. As long as he could keep on chewing gum and sifting through the facts, putting two and two together in his mind, he might come up with a brainstorm that would really help his dad find some answers.

The way things were going, he would probably go through a full crate of gum before they cracked this one—*if* they cracked it, he thought. As the paper said, there had been four kidnappings so far, and the authorities were no closer to solving them now than they had been at the start.

"It's like they never happened," his father had said one night at supper. "We know people have been kidnapped—or, more correctly, have been forced to kidnap themselves—because they tell us so when they get released. We know where they've been, how the crime was committed, but that's *it*. No clues. And since the victims never see the kidnappers....

And there it is, Mallard thought, closing his eyes — that's the part that counts. Kidnappings weren't new, but there'd been only a few that were never solved. Usually the kidnapper was traced through the ransom money or caught when the victim identified him.

In this case the victim brought the money to the kidnapper himself. The ransom was paid and the victim released before anybody even knew the crime was being committed.

The technique was always the same. It was almost too simple to believe—simple, yet apparently foolproof.

The victim would come out of his home or office, get in his car, and find a briefcase on the seat next to him. As soon as the victim was in the car, a voice would come out of the briefcase—or, actually, out of a citizens band receiver *inside* of it. The voice always said the same thing, always seemed to have the same cold quality.

"Do not move. In the briefcase are four sticks of dynamite which can be triggered electronically. We are watching you through binoculars. If you do anything wrong, we will explode the dynamite."

"You will be watched continuously," the

voice would say. "If you do not do exactly as we say, you will be blown to pieces. Nod if you understand."

At that point the voice paused for five seconds while the victim nodded. Then the victim would be instructed to go to his bank, carrying the briefcase with him. He'd be warned that if he set the briefcase down, he'd be killed. He'd be told to draw a certain amount from his account—always an amount that would not be large enough to arouse suspicion. The victim, once he was back in his car with the money, would then be instructed to drive to an isolated area, usually out in the country and always different from the site of the previous kidnapping. There he'd be told to leave the money and the briefcase. Then he'd be allowed to drive off.

Nor could the victim hang around after he left the money to try to catch a glimpse of his kidnappers. The voice always informed him that he was being covered by a high-powered rifle, was being watched through a telescopic sight, and would be killed if he didn't leave immediately. If he hesitated, as the third victim had, one shot from the rifle would make him change his mind about staying.

By the time the police arrived at the scene

the money, briefcase — everything — was gone. There were never any witnesses, no tire tracks other than the victim's—no clues at all.

"Perfect," Mallard said to himself. "The perfect crime — the do-it-yourself kidnapping."

He stood suddenly and rubbed the back of his neck. It was almost four o'clock and he was supposed to meet Rick at four-thirty. Rick Oldfield was Mallard's best friend. He was into citizens band radio and had just gotten a new rig he was anxious to show off. It was the kind that you could carry on your belt, bigger and more powerful than the hand-held kind.

"I can work clear across town," he'd told Mallard on the phone that morning. "Even hear the truckers coming in on the tollway. It's great!"

Normally Mallard wouldn't goof around in the middle of a case. But this time it was different. The kidnappings seemed to revolve around the use of a citizens band radio, and maybe if he sat down and rapped with Rick for a while, he would come up with a new twist.

"It's for sure I'm not getting anything done

around here." He snorted, balled the gum-wrapper into a wad, and threw it in the corner. Then he went outside, unlocked his ten-speed, and was into fourth by the time he hit the corner.

He snorted, balled the gum

TUNING IN ON CITIZENS BAND

"You look terrible — what's the matter?" Rick was one of those guys who always blurt out whatever they're thinking. Usually Mallard didn't mind, but this time it struck him the wrong way. He'd just fast-pedaled the ten blocks to Rick's house, and it didn't seem like much of a greeting to be criticized right away.

"Back off." He slouched into a stuffed chair in Rick's room and dug for a piece of gum.

"Pardon me for living." Rick shrugged. "It's the truth — you look rotten. Is it the kidnappings?"

Mallard nodded. "Yeah. I haven't been sleeping. Dad doesn't get home until midnight or even later, and I keep listening for him."

"No new breaks?"

"Nope. Nothing. That's why I came over.

Getting stale thinking about it. Decided I might as well get out of myself for a while." He smiled to take the sting out of his earlier grouchiness. "How's your new rig?"

"It's incredible. Far out. I was whipping around downtown day before yesterday and I just happened to go into this pawn shop. Well, this old guy had a CB rig that somebody hocked and it didn't work, so I started diddling around with it and found that the antenna was loose. That's all that was wrong. Next thing I knew he offered it to me for $20 —maybe a $70 outfit. So I wheeled home and hit Dad, and he loaned me the money."

Mallard closed his eyes, listening but not listening, thinking but not thinking — just floating. Rick finished the story of getting his new CB transceiver, and Mallard nodded without even opening his eyes.

"Man, you're really into this kidnapping thing, aren't you?" Rick squatted on the floor in front of him. "Did you hear a word I said?"

Mallard nodded. "Yeah. Just tired."

"No. It's more than that. I've seen you tired before—like when we broke that truck hijacking ring last year. This is worse. What is it?"

"Nothing — well, that's not the truth. It's Dad. I've never seen him like this. He's talking about quitting, giving up."

Rick nodded. "I thought so — it had to be something heavy. Is there anything I can do?"

"Sure. Solve the case. Other than that, I can't think of anything."

"I already told you how to solve it last week, after the fourth kidnapping. They're using CB radios, right? All you have to do is have police listening on the CB. The next job you eavesdrop and close in."

Mallard shook his head. "The FBI already thought of that. But the transmitter the kidnappers are using is really weak, maybe only half a mile range — even less. It would just be pure luck if a policeman happened to be close enough to pick up the signal. Dad's got a CB down at the station anyway — just in case."

Rick nodded. "You'd have to have a thousand smokeys to do it right." Smokey Bear was the CB nickname — "handle" — for police because some highway patrol officers wore campaign hats like Smokey the Bear's. "You know what I can't figure?"

"What?"

"How they can keep getting away with it. Four times in a row, and the victims never make a fuss, always do what they're told. You'd think just one of them would call their bluff."

"Dad talked to all the victims. He said it's the bit where they're told to open the briefcase," Mallard's voice tightened. "He says when they see that dynamite, all taped and lying there with the wire and detonator, it's like they're seeing a cobra or something. They get scared, really scared—too scared to make a fuss."

"Breaker, breaker!" A strange voice cut into the conversation, and it took Mallard a second to realize that it was only Rick's radio on the coffee table. "I've got a smokey taking pictures at mile 41 on the tollway. Watch the double nickel."

Rick smiled. "Told you it was a good rig, didn't I?"

"What was all that?"

"A trucker. He's warning other truckers that there's a highway patrol officer using radar to check speed near the 41-mile marker on the interstate coming into town."

"What's the 'double nickel'?"

"Oh, just CB for 55 miles per hour. He's telling people to watch the speed limit."

"Sounds like every trucker on the road must have a CB rig."

Rick laughed. "Not just truckers. Almost everybody else has one too. Last year when I went to the Scouting get-together at that camp down south, out of 4,000 Scouts I'll bet 90 percent had CB rigs."

"Is that right?"

"Yeah. Citizens band radio is the most popular thing going right now. It's good, too. Gives people a way to call for help if they've got an emergency or are having trouble...."

"Wait a minute. You mean there are lots of other kids in the city with CB rigs?"

"Sure. Thousands." Rick nodded. "So what?"

"Can you talk to them anytime you want?"

"Well, yeah. As long as we're on the same channel and our transmitters are powerful enough to reach each other. It's five miles all the way across the city, maybe a little more. A little hand-held rig won't reach, but a belt job like mine will..." his voice trailed off. Mallard was up and halfway to the door. "Where are you going?"

"Home. Come on. And bring your radio."

"Why are we going to your place?" Rick grabbed his CB and followed. "What's the big deal?"

"I've got an idea, and I need a map of the city. I've got one over at the house. Oh, one thing." Mallard stopped at the door. "If we should still be there when Dad comes home, it might be better if you didn't call him Smokey Bear or anything like that, all right?"

"Sure. No problem."

"The mood he's in, he might just rip your head off. So you'd better watch yourself—you know, the way you say things too fast sometimes."

"I'll try to remember," Rick said, nodding soberly as he thought of how he'd look without a head. "I really will try to remember."

CB NETWORK

"What do all the pins mean?" Rick asked.

They were back in Mallard's room, and he was looking up at a map of the city that Mallard had taped between two posters on a big piece of wallboard.

"I was trying to find a pattern for the kidnappings," Mallard explained. "The red pins are where the kidnappings took place; the blue ones are for the banks where the victims took money out of their accounts; and the green ones show where they were told to take the money and the briefcase."

Rick studied the map for a moment. "They're all *over* the place."

"Yeah. No pattern. That would have been too easy, I suppose. Still, it would have been nice. To be able to predict where they'll strike next and nail them the way we did in the truck hijacking case — that would have been all right. But these kidnappings seem to be random, at least as far as location is concerned."

"Is there anything about them that's predictable — anything you know?"

Mallard shrugged. "Well, they always pick wealthy victims. But that's the only way they could get cash so easily. You'd have to be pretty rich to walk into a bank and write a check for a couple of thousand dollars."

"I read that one of the victims was told to get only $500. Hardly seems worth all the trouble."

"Well, the way I figure it is that the kidnappers think they've got a foolproof setup, so if they get only a small amount of money but can still keep on with their racket, they're well off." Mallard was chewing gum furiously as he expounded this theory.

"Hey, I've got it!" Rick interrupted. "All we have to do is check out who the rich people are in this city and then have the police put guards on them. Then the next time the kidnappers strike, it has to be one of the people that are being watched, right?"

"Wrong." Mallard shook his head. "There's no way we could ever have that many people covered all the time. We wouldn't even be able to find out who has big money in the bank."

"So what *is* the next step?"

"Well," answered Mallard, shifting the gum from one side of his mouth to the other, "since there *is* no pattern, the way I figure is, we are going to have to make ourselves a pattern."

"With this map and pins scattered all over the place, we're going to make a pattern?"

"Right. We're going to lay out a grid."

"Grid? What kind of grid?"

"A series of overlapping areas of kids listening on CB rigs. We're going to set up a whole network. Well, that isn't quite true. *We* aren't going to do it, *you* are."

"I am?" Rick stared at him, his forehead wrinkling.

"Sure. Way it works out, if the kidnappers are using a rig that has a half-mile range, all we have to do is have a kid working a CB in each half-mile square of the city. Of course we have to figure on the worst, which means the kidnappers' rig might have an even shorter range, so we should try to have a kid every square quarter-mile. Maybe even a bit less."

"You've gone crazy." Rick had a stunned look in his eyes. "Why, there must be 10 square *miles* of city...."

"There are 14.6, to be exact, in the whole metropolitan area. But there are parks and playgrounds and the ball field, big areas where this kind of kidnapping wouldn't happen. So you can knock off the .6 and call it an even 14 square miles we've got to cover." Mallard took a pencil and drew a rough rectangle around the city map. "To be on the safe side, we should have at least two rigs working each square quarter-mile, which would be 8 per square mile. Let's see, 8 times 14...." He scratched his head.

"It's 112. You want me to get *112* rigs on the line?"

"Not exactly."

"Oh. Well, what do you want?"

"We should have enough for three shifts, really. To be sure about covering the air all the time. So you should get three times that many rigs—say 336."

"You're crazy. It can't be done." Rick dropped on the couch. "I can't just sit here and raise 300 rigs."

"That number was 336," Mallard corrected. "To be safe."

"I can't just sit here and raise 336 rigs to be safe — like I was the king of all CBers or something. You think they're just waiting out there for me to start calling? You think they're just all ready to jump in and start honking about catching the kidnappers?"

"Oh, that's another thing. I almost forgot. The kidnappers are sure to be listening to the CB channels, at least sometimes, so you'll have to have your contacts call in on the phone to find out what they're supposed to do. We don't want to blow it."

"Do you have any *idea* what you're asking?"

"Well, really, Rick — *you're* the one who was going on and on about how handy citizens band radio is; how it helps out in emergencies and all. Now's your chance to prove it."

"In spades, right?"

Mallard nodded. "Sure. Just take the map, start calling people in sectors, and have them call in on the phone to find out what you want them to do. It shouldn't be all that bad."

"No worse than watching grass grow for excitement." Rick snorted. "I ought to finish up about two and a half years from now. The kidnappers will probably be dead of old age by the time I get this thing set up."

"So you'd better start, right?" Mallard pointed a pencil at the center of the map. "The sooner we get going, the better. Here, the first block is bordered by Hampden and Twenty-first Street."

"All right, all right." Rick picked up his rig, put it on the table. "Just so you buy me some more batteries."

"Sure. We'll bill the police for them later."

"Breaker, breaker," Rick said as he triggered his mike. "This is Freckles on channel five. Breaker, breaker, somebody in the Hampden and Twenty-first Street area." He let up on the mike.

"Freckles?" Mallard looked at him.

"It's my call sign, and don't ask anything more about it." His eyes were hard.

"I wouldn't think of it."

"Hey, Freckles, breaker from Twenty-second Street. This is Shortcake. Will I do?" The radio crackled. "I'm only a block from where you asked."

"Affirmative, Shortcake, you'll do just fine," Rick answered, glowering at Mallard.

"Please call in on the phone for a private message." He gave the number. "Thanks and ten-four."

Mallard left his room to stand by the phone in the hallway, and the last thing he heard as he walked out was, "Breaker, breaker, anybody in Forty-ninth and Oak. What say, somebody, please?"

It was all he would hear for the next two days.

THE FIFTH VICTIM

"That's it, we've covered the city." Rick flopped back on the bed, his voice so hoarse it sounded like somebody pulling barbed wire through sheet metal. "And I've probably got the world's record for raising rigs."

Mallard nodded, smiled as he looked at the map. The whole city area was covered with overlapping pencil rings, each covering slightly less than a square quarter-mile. "You did an unbelievable job — I just hope it works." He joined Rick on the bed, closed his eyes, and chewed gum. Mallard, too, was talked out—he had spoken to all the CBers as they phoned in, and for the moment all he wanted to do was simply lie back and vegetate.

His room was wasted. It looked as if somebody had thrown a grenade inside and closed the door. Mallard's mother was on vacation, visiting relatives in Nebraska, so they'd eaten fast foods; when they got hungry Mallard would go down to the corner and get a pizza or hamburgers. The cartons from his trips were simply left where they'd been emptied, along with drained pop cans and milk bottles.

"This place looks like a dump," Rick had said somewhere along the line.

"Too busy to clean it," Mallard had time to blurt as the phone rang, and he ran to answer.

They'd slept when they could, in snatches, waking when somebody called in on the CB or when the phone jangled. Twice Mallard's father had come in and asked what was going on. Mallard debated whether or not to tell him the truth, that they were trying to crack the kidnapping case, but decided against it. His father had enough to do, what with the commissioner and all, and if this CB network didn't do the job, Mallard would just as soon not have his father find out about a crackpot scheme that failed.

"Rick got a new CB rig," he said. "We're doing a kind of marathon."

"Terrific! My job is coming apart on me, my

wife is away in Nebraska, and my kid spends his time doing some weird talkathon. Can't you find something more important to do?" He'd stomped out and went down to the station to be hassled by the reporters, who were on his neck like flies.

"That was bad," Rick had said, studying his friend closely. "It hurt him."

"Not nearly as much as it hurt me. But if I'd told him the truth, he either would have made us quit or brought in the police. Either way it would have killed the whole operation."

Rick had thrown him a nod. "I know, but still...."

The phone had cut in, and they'd gone back to work, the incident forgotten. But it was in the back of Mallard's mind, working at him.

It was the end of the second day. The network was practically all set up, with each area given a code number, and they were more or less just pulling loose ends together. Some of the areas didn't have enough CBers for three shifts yet, but only one area close to the park in the center of the city hadn't been covered at all.

"You know," Mallard said, rubbing the tired out of the back of his neck, "it's really hard to believe. I mean, all these people with CB rigs, and we're hitting them for help — kids, grown-ups, the whole bunch — and not one of them has turned us down. They've all been eager to help."

"That's what it's all about," Rick answered. "In a way that's the reason for CB, or anyway it's the most important reason. A way of emergency communication — a way to ask for help when you need it."

"Yeah, I know. But it's kind of hard to believe that this many people will pull together...."

"Breaker, breaker!" The radio jumped alive in the middle of his sentence. "Hey, Freckles, what's the phone line to you?"

Rick triggered the mike, gave the caller the phone number, and was about to keyoff — cut his transmitter off — when it hit him the caller hadn't given his call sign.

"Breaker back. Who is this please?" He waited a second or two, and when no answer came, he keyed his mike again. "I say again, this is Freckles on channel five — who was that last breaker, please? Would you give your call sign?"

But there was no call-back, nor did the phone ring.

"Probably just somebody who's curious," Rick said. "Or somebody who found out his sector was already covered."

"Yeah." Mallard nodded. "It could have been anything." And he'd let it go.

It was a sign that he was slipping. Normally when he was working on a case, anything out of the ordinary would cause him to become suspicious. But this time he had let it slide by. Instead of picking up on it, he had let his mind go blank and had slipped into a light doze. Now and then the CBers would check in, and he'd come half awake while Rick answered them, then go back under.

It had been hard, really hard, and their work was just starting. Now that they had the network set up, they had to wait for the kidnappers to hit again, so they could pin them down. And who knows how long that will take, he thought, in the fuzzy edge of hard sleep. It could be a week. Maybe even longer.

"Hey," Rick's voice came through like light on fog, "when did we eat last?"

"Five, maybe six hours." Mallard didn't open his eyes. "I'm not sure."

"It must be longer. I'm starving."

"You're *always* starving."

"Even so — we should eat — to keep our strength up."

Mallard sighed. "All right, I'll go get a pizza. You want plain or sausage?"

"How about one of each?" Rick mused. "And maybe some milk or a vanilla shake, and how about a side order of onion rings?"

"Onion rings and pizza?"

"Sure."

"You must have a cast-iron stomach." Mallard shook his head.

"It works just fine as long as I keep it full."

Mallard nodded and got up slowly. "I'll bet I've put 50 miles on my bike just getting pizza and hamburgers."

"It's good for you." Rick smiled. "Exercise builds character."

"Yeah." He left the room and made his way down the hallway and outside, still rubbing the sleep out of his eyes.

The bike lock on his ten-speed gave him the same old trouble. It stuck and he had to work the combination twice to loosen the tumblers, and he was just thinking about maybe buying a new lock when he heard the voice.

"Do not move. You are being watched through binoculars. If you do not do as we say, we will blow you to pieces."

Mallard froze. The voice was cold, hard, and even, and he cast about trying to find the source. It took him just a few seconds of letting his eyes move to find it.

The briefcase was just to his right, stuck between two garbage cans, its brown leather glistening in the evening sun. Attached to the handle was a set of handcuffs with one of the bracelets left open.

"Nod if you understand us."

He stared at the briefcase. His throat was suddenly dry, tight. He could feel the sweat start to pour from his forehead. It was just four feet from his head—four incredibly short feet. One wrong move and there wouldn't be enough of him left to find and bury. He'd be more than dead. He'd be *gone*.

Slowly, ever so slowly—his life hanging on the movement—Mallard nodded his head.

VOICE FROM THE BRIEFCASE

"Now stand, slowly."

Mallard did as he was told, rising from where he'd been kneeling by the lock. Every fiber in his whole body wanted to *run*, to turn and bolt for safety. But he knew he wouldn't make two steps.

"Pick up the briefcase."

Pick it *up*? His mind screamed—pick it up and *hold* it? Pick up that filthy piece of death and hold it *next* to me? He hesitated.

"Pick up the briefcase. *Now*. Or you will die."

It was the coldness of the voice that made him move. It was so impersonal, so even and still that he felt it could kill him and not care in the least, could kill like a snake. In a flash he remembered how one of the victims had compared his experience to sitting down next to a cobra.

He moved, picked up the briefcase, and was strangely surprised to find it fairly heavy. He didn't know dynamite was so heavy.

"Now put the open handcuff on your wrist."

He complied, left it loose.

"Tighter."

Man, he thought, they are watching me like a hawk! He looked around the neighborhood, trying to see where they were watching from, but noticed nothing out of the ordinary. Down the block there were several cars parked; they could be watching from one of them, but he couldn't see inside the cars.

"Now open the briefcase."

Again he hesitated. He didn't want to see it, not really. It was enough to know it was there.

"Do it *now*."

He nodded and put the briefcase across the handlebars of his bike. It took a second or two of juggling — it was awkward because of the handcuff — but he finally clicked the thumb-hasp and opened the lid.

Inside lay four sticks of dynamite, four yellow-paper and waxen tubes of death bonded together with black electrical tape.

Next to the dynamite were two small CB radios. One of them was a receiver and the other one served as a transmitter, so when he spoke they could hear him. There was a two-way speaker built into the case.

"You'll never get away with this," Mallard said into the second CB rig. "You don't have a chance."

"Shut up." The answer was immediate and hard. "If you speak again, you will die."

Do this I die, he thought, do that I die—it's getting so I can't do anything. Some of the fear was going away now, not much, but enough to let his mind work. They weren't going to kill him, at least not right away. If they had wanted to kill him, they would have just triggered the charge when he kneeled down to unlock his bike.

No, they were saving him for something ...but *what*? What did he have that they wanted? Certainly not ransom money. Why didn't they just drop him right off?

Rick!

That was it—they must be waiting to get Rick into it as well. They wanted the two of them. If they just got rid of Mallard and left Rick, the CB network would still be able to operate.

As if on cue, at the worst possible moment, Rick came running out of the house.

"I heard it all on the CB — for a minute I couldn't make the connection. It threw me. Then I knew it had to be you...." He trailed off, staring at the briefcase, his feet slowing.

"You *had* to come." Mallard sighed. "I don't suppose you called the police first?"

"No. It took me a second or two to figure out what was going on — that it was happening right outside. It didn't make any sense at first...."

"You — the second boy. Come over to your bicycle." The voice cut in. "Do it *now*."

Rick stopped. "That's them?"

Mallard nodded. "The kidnappers."

"Now they've got us both."

"So it appears."

"I blew it, right?"

"I couldn't have put it better myself." Mallard shrugged.

"Approach your bicycle." The voice came out of the briefcase. "If you do not do so at once, we will trigger the charge."

"All right, all right, keep your shirt on." Rick went over to his bike.

"Unlock it."

Rick leaned down and worked the combination lock. It popped free.

"Now, listen, both of you. You will get on your bikes and ride south to Elm Street. There you will turn right and ride until you come to the edge of the city. Do you understand?"

They nodded. "What then?" Rick asked.

"You will be given further instructions at that time. Now start riding."

Mallard, after having some trouble fastening the handcuff, finally got started. Rick followed slightly to the left and rear.

They rode silently for almost two blocks, getting through the gears. At the third block Rick pulled up alongside.

"How'd they find us?"

"That strange call." Mallard forced a smile, but there was no humor in it. "This afternoon —the guy who asked for the phone number. It must have been one of the kidnappers. Man, what a sap I was not to figure the kidnappers might be picking up your CB calls and would find out what we were doing."

"You couldn't think of everything."

"But it was stupid to miss that...."

"Shut up. Both of you. Ride silently." The

voice chopped into the middle of a sentence.

Mallard stopped talking, but after they'd ridden another block, Rick came up alongside again. "What do you think they'll do with us?"

Mallard didn't answer — for two reasons. One, they'd hear him and it wouldn't do any good to give them ideas. Two, it didn't seem necessary to bring Rick down, didn't seem right to tell him that the kidnappers could blow them both up, let the network die down for a couple of weeks, then go right back to their operation. With Rick and Mallard out of the way, the whole CB plan would come apart.

There was no sense bringing it up, no sense answering Rick. One way or the other, he'd find out what was going to happen pretty soon.

And for now they couldn't do anything but ride where they were told, monotonously pump the pedals while Mallard tried to formulate a plan, get his brain working.

All they had to do was ride — with 14 pounds of death hanging from Mallard's wrist.

TRAPPED IN THE DARK

Three blocks passed by, then four and five, and Mallard tore his brain apart, trying to come up with a way to escape.

I should have run, he thought, when I first saw the briefcase. I should have chanced it and split. But even as the thought entered his mind he remembered the cold horror that had passed through him when he saw the leather case; the stunning, mind-freezing, raw *fear* that had pinned him like a bug in a collection.

If only Rick had called the police! Or if the kidnapping had occurred somewhere else, so it would have been picked up by someone in the network. But no, Rick couldn't be blamed —he had simply come to help when he heard it all on the CB. He'd just done what Mallard would have done.

If only, if only, if only—it went through his mind like a chant, a stupid song, and no thoughts came, nothing he could use.

In the seventh block, he signaled Rick to come up alongside again. When he looked back to make the motion he saw a car, four blocks back. It might have been the kidnappers following them. It was dark blue, an older model, and he studied it for a moment, but then it turned off. Later a small tan car seemed to hang back behind the bikes as though it might be tailing them. Either they were switching cars or they were following further back. Or even driving up ahead someplace.

"What's cooking?" Rick whispered so it wouldn't be picked up by the mike in the briefcase.

Mallard moved his head to the side and spoke as low as he could. "When we get to the next corner, take off to the side. Split. Get away from me—they won't follow you."

"No." Rick shook his head emphatically. "No way—they'll blow you away."

"Better just one than two," Mallard hissed. "You take off."

"*No*. We're in this together, all the way." This time Rick forgot and spoke aloud, and he'd no sooner gotten the words out than the briefcase came alive.

"No more talk. Next time we trigger the charge."

The boys became quiet again, and Rick dropped back slightly. They hit Elm Street still riding in silence, and Mallard turned right and headed west out of town.

It was two miles to the edge of the city, two of the longest miles Mallard had ever ridden. He was breathing much harder than such a short ride would normally make him breathe. It amazed him that of all the people they passed — of all the *hundreds* of people — not one seemed to think it strange that a boy would be riding through town handcuffed to a leather briefcase.

He wanted to scream at them, scream that he was scared and carrying death, but he feared that if he opened his mouth the transmitter in the briefcase would pick it up.

He did try to get the attention of the people they passed. He took his free hand from the handlebar to make small waves and point to the leather case; once he even tried a low whistle, but nobody paid any attention. Or, if they did, they simply dismissed it as the antics of a crazy kid and ignored it.

Finally, as they neared the edge of the city, it came to Mallard that the transmitter in the briefcase might be his salvation. If the people on the network were listening, maybe they would hear what he and Rick had said, or they might hear him now and pick up on what was happening.

"Dynamite." He leaned down to the briefcase to where it lay across the handlebars. "Dynamite, dynamite, dynamite...."

"One more word and we trigger."

He closed his mouth. But maybe he'd gotten through, maybe they'd heard. It was at least something to hope for, to think about as they rode.

At the edge of the city, he slowed. This is it, he thought, this is where they dust us off. The road was lined with trees, and there wasn't much traffic — an occasional car or truck. It would be the perfect place to get rid of them.

"Take off, Rick!" he turned and screamed. "Make for the brush, *now*!"

But Rick wouldn't leave him, and instead of getting blown to smithereens, as he was sure he would, he heard the voice come on again.

"Do as you're told and you won't be hurt." This time it sounded less hard, more reassuring. "We have no desire to kill, just detain you. Keep riding for two more miles, until you see a dirt road off to the right. Take it."

It struck Mallard that their pursuers were sure being talkative, but then he remembered that the CB network covered only the city and they were now well out of town. Nobody would pick them up.

Still, perhaps the kidnappers weren't lying. Maybe they really weren't going to kill the boys, just hold them for a few days; it would probably take two days for the network to die down, then they'd have another day to work the kidnapping to pick up more money.

All guesswork, he thought, pedaling slowly as they came to a grade. He geared down to fifth and heard Rick's chain linkage click as he did the same.

It was dusk, almost soft dark, when they came to the dirt road. Mallard turned right and found himself on what amounted to an old logging trail that led back into the woods.

He slowed, then stopped, and Rick stopped beside him.

"What do you think?" Rick's voice had a tremor to it. "Are they going to kill us?"

"You will not be killed." The briefcase answered. "A mile down this road there is an old sawmill. There you will find a tool storage shed. Park your bikes there and wait."

The boys started again. The ruts in the road were soft dirt, and the narrow wheels on their ten-speeds sank in and made it hard going. It took them almost half an hour to cover the mile, and when they finally got to the clearing by the old sawmill, it was dark, and they were both winded.

On one side of the clearing, nestled back in the darkness, Mallard could make out a small shed. It was the only building standing, so he figured it was the tool shed they'd been told about, and he went to it and laid his bike down.

For a moment the two boys stood. It was strange; they were alone, yet not alone because of the briefcase.

Presently they heard the noise of a car coming down the road. There were no lights, and the car stopped back around a bend so they couldn't see it.

"Stay right where you are standing." The voice was loud, much louder than it had been, so the transmitter must be in the car, close. Just as Mallard had thought. "You will find a key for the handcuffs under the stone slab just to the left of the door. Remove the brief-case and put it and the key outside the door, then get inside and close the door, and be quick about it!"

Smooth, Mallard thought. Like velvet. Without the dynamite and briefcase there would be no evidence, no way to tie the crime to the criminals.

Still, they had no choice. If they didn't do as told, the kidnappers could still trigger the charge. The dynamite would probably blow the shed and them to kingdom come before they took a step.

Together Rick and Mallard lifted the heavy slab of stone. Rick grabbed the key and un-locked the handcuffs, and Mallard was finally free of the heavy weight of the briefcase. It felt so good that for a moment he relaxed, untensed his body, and massaged his sore wrist. The voice, angrier now — forcing Mallard back under its control, came crackling through the quiet.

"Now get inside, and shut the door. Quick!" They were sure watching every little move, Mallard thought.

Rick and Mallard entered the shed as they were told to do, closed the door, and waited.

It was pitch black inside. Pretty soon they heard footsteps approaching and a rattling noise as a lock was put on the door.

Then they heard a low laugh. "Man, you kids — you almost blew it for us. If I hadn't happened to pick up on those calls you were making...."

"Shut up." A second voice cut him off.

"Yeah. I know, talk doesn't do any good," the first voice answered. "Listen in there: you can't get out. We beefed the place up and repaired it just for this kind of emergency. I'll be on guard and bring you food and water in the morning. Do you understand?"

"Yeah." Mallard put his head down by the door. "But you can't get away with it. No way. Why don't you just let us go?"

"You're wrong," the voice answered. "We already have gotten away with it."

That was the last of the communication. The boys heard the sound of the car engine revving up and the car backing around, then it died as the car moved down the trail.

Now all they could do was wait.

ESCAPE

For a moment the two boys simply stood in the blackness of the shed. It was so dark that their eyes couldn't get used to it; after several minutes they still couldn't see anything, couldn't even make out shadows.

"I've got some matches," Rick said. "Should I light one?"

Mallard didn't answer. Rick could hear him rustling in his pockets and decided to light a match anyway.

In the sudden flare he could see that they were in a simple, empty, boxlike room; all heavy boards nailed to massive timbers. It was about as stout as a tank, and there were no windows.

Out of the corner of his eye, just as the

match flame died, he could see Mallard had found what he'd been digging for in his pockets.

It was a very limp stick of gum.

"Ahh." Rick nodded, suddenly plunged back into the darkness. He lit another match and saw that Mallard had settled into the corner in a squat and was chewing his gum intensely. "*Now* you're going to think, right? Now that we're locked in and they've got us where they want us — *now* you're going to think."

"Shut up, Rick."

"The kidnappers fell right into our trap, right? You had it all planned this way, right?"

"Rick...."

Rick closed his mouth. Talking wouldn't do any good anyway, and he realized bugging Mallard was just a way to let off steam. Another match died. Rick felt his way to the wall and slouched down.

In the blackness the only sound was the rhythmic chewing of Mallard's gum and their breathing. After a time Rick caught himself dozing, fought it for a moment, and then decided to heck with it, and let sleep come over him.

He wasn't sure how long he'd slept — it

could have been a few minutes or an hour—when Mallard shook him awake.

"Come on, Rick. Wake up!" Mallard whispered.

He opened his eyes, struggled to see, and then remembered where they were. "What's wrong?"

"I've got it!"

"Got what?"

"How they work—what the kidnappers are doing. I've got it."

"Sure, so have I. They kidnap people and demand money. It's pretty simple."

"No! *This*, what they're doing with us—it didn't make any sense. What good did it do them, really, to kidnap us? The listening network would still be there."

"Sure." Rick's mind was starting to work. "But the CBers would call in, and we wouldn't be there."

"Yeah, but they know the scoop. When they can't get us, they call the police—either way the job gets done."

"Well then, like you say, what good did it do to take us?"

"Not *us*. *Me*."

"I don't follow."

"Well, first I figure the kidnappers called in

the way the rest of the CBers did. It was easy enough for them to pick up on one of the calls you made, then telephone and find out what it was all about without ever identifying themselves."

"Right. Then they called the phone company to find out where that number was."

"Wrong. They'd never get an address just by asking for it. And there's no way they'd have time to cross-check to find it in the phone book. When they set up that CB-rigged briefcase near my bike, they never knew we were the ones who were setting up the CB network. All they knew was that that was the address where Inspector Westerman lived, and they must have figured at least one of the bikes belonged to me and that sooner or later I'd come out and walk into their trap."

"So how come they waited for me to come out if they didn't know we were both involved in the CB plan?"

"Because they couldn't be sure which one of us was Inspector Westerman's son, and with both bikes there, they couldn't afford to take a chance and pick up the wrong kid."

"So now they've got us both, but what's the difference? If one of the CBers calls in to tell how they heard you shouting 'Dynamite' into the transmitter, the police will be on their tail anyhow."

"Not so," Mallard corrected. "When a CBer calls in to report, who does he call?"

"The smokey in charge of the kidnapping investigation. They'd wind up talking to—"

"My father," Mallard finished for him. "That's who's in charge of the investigation. And what if the kidnappers do get tracked down that way, the way we planned? All they have to do is send a radio message that lets Dad know who it is they're holding, that they've got *me* captive. What if they tell him they'll blow us to pieces if he does anything?"

"His hands are tied." Rick nodded in the darkness. "He'd be afraid to do anything."

"Exactly. And the kidnappers will have made one more score. I'll bet anything this is a big one too, bigger than the rest, because they'll never dare try another kidnapping." He smacked a fist into his palm. "We've got to get out of here, got to get word to Dad somehow."

"Not to be snotty, but it may have slipped your mind that we're locked in what amounts to a jail, and there's a guard rumbling around outside someplace." Rick snorted. "Of course, other than that, it's duck soup."

"Light a match." Mallard cut him off. "I want to look around again."

"All right. But it won't do any good. I looked, and this place is some *kind* of strong."

"Just do it."

Rick fumbled for a match and struck it. In the yellow glow Mallard gave the room a quick once-over. When the first match went out he made Rick light a second, and this time he pointed to a spot high on the back wall. "Right there."

"Right there what?" It was simply a spot like any other—just another heavy board.

"That's where we're going to get out. Sort of."

"But it's impossible. That's heavy timber. There's no way we can get through that."

"Sure. *You* know that, and *I* know that, but does the guy outside know that? If we start hammering right there, slow and steady, with our fists and *keep* hammering there, what do you think will happen?"

"He'll shoot us?" Rick offered helpfully. "Through the walls?"

"No. At least I don't think so. At first he won't do anything, but if we take turns and keep at it, sooner or later he's going to think we know something he doesn't — he'll *think* we're getting out. He's going to have to open that door to stop us, or to see what we're really doing. And right then...."

"He'll shoot us?" Rick repeated. "Through the open doorway?"

"No. Right then, when he pulls the door open, we run out and split, one each way. One of us has to get away, the way I see it. Maybe both. As soon as we're free, we call Dad and tell him it's all right to bust them."

Mallard turned and started pounding, a steady, slow thumping — thump, thump, thump. When his right hand got tired, he switched to his left, and when they both got tired, he whispered to Rick to take over.

For quite some time, nothing happened, and Mallard began to wonder whether there even *was* a guard, whether it had all been a trick. But no, finally a voice came through the closed door.

"Hey, in there — knock that off. You can't get out."

The boys remained silent, kept thumping.

"I told you to stop it!"

Thump, thump, thump.

"I'll count to five, and if you haven't

stopped I'm going to shoot through the walls."

"I *told* you." Rick hissed.

"Keep knocking — it's working. He can't stand it." Mallard took over and kept up the same even pace.

"One, two, three, four, five." He counted fast, and Rick felt his muscles tense, waiting for the shot.

Still Mallard pounded, a steady, nerve-grating pounding like the old Chinese water torture.

No shots came. In fact for another long period nothing happened.

Then came the magic sound of metal on metal as the guard worked the key into the lock, a faint clicking that could just barely be heard over the pounding.

"Get ready! Over there, by the door!" Mallard breathed the warning into Rick's ear. "You go left and I'll go right."

The lock came free and the boys could hear the rasp of a metal bolt being pulled back.

Come *on*, Rick thought, get it over with, get the door *open*. He tightened his leg muscles, crouched by the door, waiting for what seemed like hours.

Finally a tiny crack of light — not daylight but moonlight — appeared as the door moved open.

"NOW!"

Mallard's scream was like an explosion, a bomb going off in Rick's ear, and without thinking he leaped up and piled himself into the opening door.

END OF THE "PERFECT" CRIME

They were through and out of the shack!

The door slammed open as though it had been hit by a truck. And they were through and running, running like they'd never run before, running for their lives, when it dawned on Mallard that something had gone wrong, something unexpected that didn't make any sense.

He slowed his wild run and looked back.

Nothing. Nobody was following him, nor had anybody gone after Rick, who was running in the opposite direction.

He stopped and turned around. Squinting, he could make out the shack in the faint moonlight, the door still hanging open. But he couldn't see a person of any kind, and it took him a full minute of cautious staring to make out a huddled form on the ground behind and partially under the door.

"Hey, Rick!" he yelled in the direction Rick had run. "Come on back. It's all right. We knocked the guy out with the door."

"Are you sure?" The answer came from a good hundred yards into the brush on the other side of the shed.

"Yeah. Come on back."

Mallard approached the still form carefully. It was so *small*. It looked like a miniature human, and when he got closer he could see why.

It was an old man. Even in the pale moonlight, it was easy to see he was probably close to seventy-five, old and wrinkled and out as cold as a mackerel from getting slammed by the door.

Bending down, Mallard could see a knot on the old man's forehead where the door had hit him, and even as he watched the man moaned.

This was the kidnapper's guard? This was the man they'd picked to keep the boys captive?

"Why—it's an old man!" Rick came up behind him, panting. "What—"

"Don't know." Mallard worked quickly because the old man was coming around. He pulled the guy's belt loose. "Help me tie him, just in case. And look for his gun—if he even has one. This is getting weirder by the minute."

They tied the old man's hands in back of him and searched carefully all around for a gun. As Mallard has suspected, there wasn't one.

"This is insane." Rick stood over the man. "What could they be thinking of to leave a grandfather behind."

"Nobody left me anywhere, sonny." The old man looked up at them from the ground. *"I'm* the one who does the leaving. And watch your manners, boy, when you speak to your elders."

"Sorry," Rick said automatically. Then he slapped his forehead. "Listen to me — I'm apologizing to somebody who almost killed me."

"Didn't neither. You just thought I would, and you'd have kept on thinking that too—if you hadn't been so lamebrained stupid as to start that thumping. And me with a headache too. Here, help me up."

Mallard and Rick leaned down and helped

him to a sitting position. The old man rested his head against the wall. A big lump was growing on his forehead where the door had struck him.

"Wait a minute!" Mallard threw up his hands. "This is starting to come through."

"You the smart one?" The old man looked at him sharply. "You the one who started the pounding?"

Mallard nodded. "And you...."

"Yup — it figures you'd catch on. I'm the kidnapper you've been after."

"The *only* one, right?"

The gray head nodded. "Yup. The one and only — you done busted up the whole ring, right here."

"You mean to tell me that this is the guy who's done all the kidnapping?" Rick laughed. "This old guy? You're kidding."

"You just untie me, and I'll show you who's kidding, bush-tail."

"But we heard two voices outside the shed. And then another voice on the CB rig. You mean that was you, too?"

"That it was, boy." He changed his voice so that it sounded like one of the men outside the shed. "I used to work in radio. Sometimes I'd play three or four different parts at the same time."

"It's true." Rick's mouth dropped open when he heard the voices. "It *was* you, all the time—it was your voice with the dynamite."

"'Tweren't dynamite. Just modeling clay with yellow wax paper. Looked good, though, didn't it?"

"Where's the car?" Rick looked around. "Somebody drove the car away."

"I did. It's back around the bend. Then I walked back. I was going to stay outside the shed till morning, to make sure you were all right, then I had one more job to do, so I figured to tell the cop I had his kid. Use it to keep him from doing anything."

"That's about how I had it figured." Mallard nodded. "At least that part of it. Of course, I thought there were two or three people involved. I didn't know it was just one old—" He was going to say "old man," but changed his mind. "I didn't know it was just you."

"Old man—that's what you were going to say. That's why I did it, you know."

"Because you're old?"

"Yup. At least partly. See, you wouldn't

know what it's like for us old radio actors. We had the best of everything. Used to be plays on every radio station—daytime and evening shows too. Now all it is is music and news. All the good stuff is on TV. But even they don't know what real acting is. You don't find many actors like me who could play different parts and have people believe it's more than one person. No place for that on TV."

"Well, you don't have to work anymore, anyhow, do you?" Mallard hoped his question wouldn't make the old man angry again, but he was obviously way past retirement age, no matter how great he had been in his prime.

"You just don't know how it is," the old man answered with a sad note in his voice. "I figured before I cashed in my chips, I just had to do it one more time—show the world that I could still give a good performance. Nobody wants to hire me now. But I figured out a way I could write my show, play all the parts, and even direct the action."

"Are you telling me you did it all just to make a big impression? So why did you make all those people get money out of their bank accounts and deliver it to you? That's not play-acting. That's a crime!"

"I know that, sonny. But if I didn't actually make them give up the money, they could always say afterwards that I wasn't convincing. I never meant to keep the money. Heck, my pension is enough for the way I live."

"Well, what did you do with all the money then?" Mallard decided he'd better take charge of the investigation and get all the information his father would need.

"It's all back there in the car," the old man answered. "And you can count it. You'll find it's all there, right down to the last cent."

"Is your CB transmitter in the car too?" Mallard asked.

"Sure is. It looks like a weak set, but I have a linear amplifier that will boost the power way up."

"Linear amps aren't legal on CB sets," said Rick. "But I guess neither is kidnapping."

Mallard sighed and turned to Rick. "See if you can raise someone on his radio—tell them we've broken the kidnapping ring."

Rick was gone before he's finished the sentence, and Mallard let himself slide down the wall next to the old man. He was tired, so exhausted even his feet ached.

It was over, over and done. But something

was bothering him. "Look, you know I've got to turn you in, don't you?

The old man nodded.

"I mean I can't just let you go."

"Look, boy, I know what's bothering you. I'm an old man, and I'll probably get some time in prison for this — though juries have been known to be easy on old people. But don't let it worry you. I knew what I was doing before I started."

"But you sound so cheerful about it all."

"Sure. I almost got away with it, the perfect performance. It would have been too—if you hadn't started that network and brought me out in the open. That was a smooth move."

Mallard shrugged. "I just did what seemed right at the time."

"And that's a pretty good way to live, boy, a pretty good way to live."

"I got through." Rick came back. "That rig of his," he pointed to the old man, "is all right. I raised the police station on channel nine easily, and it just took a minute to get your dad on the line. Only—"

"Only what?" Mallard looked up. "I don't like that tone."

"Well, he sounded pretty mad about us

being involved in the kidnappings and all. I mean really mad, except he *was* glad we're all right. And I was just getting him smoothed down when I blew it."

"How?"

"I called him Smokey Bear. I'm really sorry, but it just slipped out."

"Oh, great. Just great. I solve the perfect crime and my dad is going to kill me. That's all I need."

You think you've got it rough." Rick sat down next to Mallard. "*I've* got to raise more than 300 rigs all over again and tell all those people we don't need them after all. Besides, your dad will probably forget being mad, what with the jewel robbery."

"Jewel robbery?" Mallard turned to him, keeping his eye on the old man. "What jewel robbery?"

"I don't know much about it. When I told your dad we'd cracked the kidnapping case, he said he was glad because it would give him more time for the jewel robbery. Somebody broke into the Museum of Art and took about $1 million worth of antique jewelry. He said there weren't any clues."

"No clues, you say?"

Rick looked at him. "Oh, no you don't. I know that sound in your voice."

"Over $1 million and no clues?"

"Aww, c'mon, Mal, not *again!*"

But he knew it was too late. Too late by a mile.

Mallard was probing his pockets, looking for another stick of gum.

THE CURSE OF THE COBRA

A Mystery

by Gary Paulsen

cover by Monroe Eisenberg

SCHOLASTIC INC.
New York Toronto London Auckland Sydney Tokyo

ISBN: 0-590-12081-6

12 11 10 9 8 7 6 5 4 3   4 5 6 7 8/8

Printed in the U.S.A.   01

CONTENTS

THE CURSE REVEALED

Malcolm — nicknamed Mallard — Westerman had been to the museum of art twice before. Both times he had stayed only long enough to get what he needed to finish his papers and left at once. It wasn't that he hated art; he hadn't really developed an interest in it.

This time it was different. Mallard was working on a case, and a case that by all outward signs might prove impossible to solve.

This time when he entered the museum with his father and Rick, he stopped just inside the door and studied the place as he would study any crime site.

The huge building was the city's pride, an immense concrete structure with tall, narrow windows, tiered hallways, and high, vaulted ceilings.

"It's like going to the bottom of the ocean," Rick whispered. "Makes me want to hold my breath."

Mallard agreed but didn't answer. The walls were painted a soft blue, and the way the light hit them did produce a slightly aquatic effect.

"You kids stay out of the way," Mallard's father ordered, moving off toward the jewelry wing. "I don't want you getting into things."

Mallard watched him go, waited until he was out of sight, then grabbed Rick by the arm with a brisk "Come on!" He hurried down the hall, and Rick had to trot to keep up.

When they reached the jewelry wing, Mallard moved off to the side so his father wouldn't notice him. "Just want to study the situation," he said, leaning against the wall and sliding a stick of gum — he'd bought another pack in the entryway machines—into his mouth. His eyes were half closed, and he chewed slowly.

"Well, that's that." Rick shrugged. "You'll stay in that trance for an hour."

Rick left Mallard standing there and edged toward the center of the huge room. Glass

cases full of antique jewelry lined the sides of the gallery. A large, free-standing case in the center was surrounded by police, museum officials, and security guards. They all looked worried, and as Rick moved closer he could overhear their conversation.

"A million dollars. That's what it was worth." The curator of the museum, a short, slightly overweight man, was talking to Mallard's father. "The amulet of King Kofren, pharaoh in the Fourth Dynasty — forty-five hundred years ago. It was made of gold, set with rubies and emeralds."

"Do you have any pictures of it?" Mallard's dad was trying to pacify the curator.

"It was worth a cool million, and I want to know what the police are going to do about it!"

"Again, do you have a picture of it?"

"Of course I have! What kind of museum do you think I'm running here? We have everything documented — documented and well guarded. Or at least that's what I thought."

"May I have a picture now?" Rick could see that the inspector was barely holding his temper. "So I can get it out to my officers?"

The head of the museum nodded, and one of

the guards went for the picture. Rick moved as close to the group as he dared.

"Now," Inspector Westerman made his voice cool and calm, "let's go over it one more time. Did anybody see *anything*?"

The head of the museum looked at him. "No. Somebody came in here in broad daylight, with guards all over the place, with security systems locked into the case — electronic warning devices wired, not only to the case, but to the amulet itself—and walked out with it. Nobody saw a thing. I just told you. In fact that makes the *third* time I've told you. And I want to know what the police intend to do about it."

The guard returned with several copies of the museum catalog and passed them around. Rick got his hands on one and moved back away, over to where Mallard stood, still chewing gum.

Rick looked at the table of contents and turned to the page about the amulet. There was a full-color picture, showing a piece of jewelry about four inches across, shaped like a bursting sun, with a gold neckpiece in the shape of two cobras which clasped around the wearer's neck.

"Wow—it's beautiful." He held the picture

out to Mallard, who took the catalog.

"Yeah." Mallard smiled. "Beautiful and expensive." He handed the catalog back to Rick and returned to his study of the room.

"Don't you want to know more about the amulet?" Rick asked.

"No," Mallard sighed. "It doesn't really matter — what they stole isn't as important as the crime."

"Still — there's some stuff written here under the picture. It might help."

Mallard smiled. "All right, what does it say?"

Rick scanned it quickly. "It belonged to King Kofren and was supposed to give him the power of the sun. The cobra neckpiece is for protection—the two cobras are supposed to protect whoever wears it, make him immortal and godlike. Oh—"

Rick stopped for a moment, and Mallard turned to him. "Oh, what? What's the matter?"

"There's a curse on the amulet."

"You're kidding — that's too corny." Mallard laughed. "A curse—really?"

"Yeah. I guess it's written right on the back of the sunburst part."

"What does it say?"

"'Whosoever shall use the power of this amulet wrongly shall die of the cobra's sting,'" Rick read aloud. Then he grabbed his throat and threw one hand in the air. "The curse of the mummy — arrgh! To die of the cobra's sting, kicking and squirming!"

"Yeah." Mallard gave him a smile and went back to work. Kidding around didn't get the job done, Mallard thought. There was nothing like plain old work.

Of course, that was before the curse came true.

SHARP OPERATORS

Most crimes are solved by following normal police procedure — dusting for fingerprints, tracking down eyewitness reports, checking places that deal in stolen goods.

As Mallard and Rick stood to the side in the museum, Inspector Westerman put his department's machinery in gear. Police officers were dispatched, all-points bulletins were sent out, known dealers in stolen jewelry were listed, and officers sent to question them.

But there are some cases where normal procedure doesn't work. They are rare, but all cities have files of unsolved cases — some dating back twenty years. When such a case

comes up, there are only two ways to solve it. Either pure luck comes into play — and a break occurs that isn't expected — or abnormal procedures have to be followed.

Mallard suspected that this case wouldn't be solved by normal police methods. He watched the fingerprint experts dusting the case for prints and knew they wouldn't find anything even before they turned to his father and shook their heads.

Whoever pulled this one wouldn't leave prints. The criminal was too sharp for that, too sharp and smooth.

Finally the area around the case cleared as officers went off to their assignments. Mallard's father was alone with the head of the museum, who was still ranting about the police; Mallard made his way to them. Rick followed, museum catalog in hand.

"Hi, Dad." Mallard came up alongside the case. "How's it going?"

"Oh, hi." His father turned. "I forgot that you were here. It's a stickler, this one — no clues. At least, there aren't any so far."

"Who's this kid?" The museum director looked at Mallard as though he might be one of the crooks.

"My son." The inspector let an edge come

into his voice. "He was with me when I got the call about the theft."

"So you brought him right along." The curator's voice was sarcastic. "Are they letting kids join the force these days?"

"Look, mister, I've been nice until now." Mallard's father turned to face him. "Maybe you'd better cool down before I arrest you for disorderly."

"All right, all right." The curator smiled and shrugged. "I'm sorry — I know how I've been acting. But this could ruin our reputation as a museum. People will be afraid to lend us material for exhibition if we can't offer more protection than this." He pointed at the empty glass case. "And we don't even know how they did it."

Mallard held up his hand. "Excuse me, sir, but that isn't quite true."

"I *knew* you had something." Rick slapped Mallard on the shoulder. "When you half closed your eyes."

"What do you mean?" The curator looked sharply at Mallard.

"I mean we have a good idea as to how it was done. But that doesn't bring us any closer to catching the thieves—except that we know a little about them."

"How did they do it?" Mallard's father studied him. "Since *we* have a pretty good idea, you might as well clue me in."

"The truth is that the security measures around the amulet weren't all that good." Mallard shot a glance at the curator, who started to say something then stopped. "There was a glass case over the amulet," Mallard continued, "but it was easy to lift. Other than that, there was just the wire from the amulet to the alarm system, but that could have been cut with a fingernail clipper."

"Wait a minute." The curator held up his hand. "Aren't you forgetting a couple of things? There were guards in the room, and the glass case was surrounded by a series of electronic light beams that went from floor to ceiling. The beams are only three inches apart, and if they're broken by any object, they set off the alarm."

"That's not quite true. If the beams are broken by any object but another light source, they'll set off the alarm. But the photoeyes in the floor are set to receive light —*any* light. Anybody shining a tiny flashlight down into them could have reached right through, lifted the glass case, snipped the

wire, and taken the amulet. The electric eyes wouldn't have known the difference — wouldn't even have sensed that the beam was broken, since the flashlight beam took the place of the regular one."

Mallard's father looked at him. "How did you figure all this out? I've been standing right here and it didn't hit me."

"But you were being pressured by folks." Mallard smiled. "Besides, I read a detective story just last week in which a man cheated some light beams to break into a bank. Maybe the crook read the same story."

"Aren't you forgetting something?" the head of the museum interrupted them. "What about all the guards—there were three right here in this room all the time. How did the crook take the amulet without being seen?"

"Yes. Well." Mallard coughed. "It might be possible that if you checked you would find that all three guards *weren't* in the room at the same time. Then, too, the job could have been done in less than five seconds. I'm sure if we go back over it we'll find that something happened to distract the guards for a few seconds."

"The kid is right," one of the guards cut in.

He'd been standing on the other side of the case and came around. "Joe was out of the room for five minutes—on a nature call. During that time only three or four people came through to look at the amulet."

Mallard turned to him. "Did something happen to make you look away for a few seconds?"

"No—wait a minute. Yeah, while Joe was gone somebody out in the hallway dropped a load of change on the floor. The money was rattling all over the place, and we looked away."

"That's it!" Mallard nodded. "That's when they took it. How long after that did you notice that the amulet was gone?"

The guard frowned, remembering. "Maybe ten minutes, a little less. Joe came back, and it was a few minutes after that when I looked over at the case and saw it was gone. Not more than ten minutes."

"All right. Now think back and try to remember the last person you saw at the glass case, looking at the amulet."

Again the guard frowned. "Let's see, there was an older woman, then a young woman, then a man with gray hair, and then a kind of fat man in a green suit. Yeah, that was the

last. The overweight guy in the green suit. He was the one."

"Probably." Mallard nodded. "We can't be sure, but that sounds about right." He smiled grudgingly in admiration. "Pretty slick — a well-planned operation, all the way."

Mallard's father turned to a passing uniformed officer. "Put an APB out on a fat guy in a green suit. Get all the particulars from the guard." He turned back to Mallard, who was looking carefully around the edge of the glass case.

"Thanks for the help," he offered.

"Well, as I said, you were being pressured and couldn't really study the situation. I had more time."

"Thanks, anyway. What are you doing now?"

"Oh. Well, the thief had to lift the glass case without leaving prints, and he couldn't very well do it with rubber gloves. They'd show him up right away. My guess is that he had airplane model cement on his fingers — yes, here are some pieces of dried glue. See, right here?"

"Sure enough." Mallard's father found the traces of dried glue. "The thief was sharp, all right, having an accomplice drop the coins at the right time. Still, we should catch them before long. As soon as they try to sell the amulet, we'll nail them."

Mallard didn't answer and instead dropped back away from the case. Rick came to his side.

"Well, cracked another one, didn't you?" Rick smiled. "I suppose now you'll get cocky —won't talk to your old friends. This must be the record, cracking a case in fifteen minutes."

Mallard smiled. "It isn't cracked. I have a strange feeling about this one."

"What do you mean?"

"I don't know, exactly. Just a strange feeling down in my guts." He put his glasses, which he'd lowered to study the glass case, back up on top of his head and started for the door. "Just a strange feeling," he repeated. "We're not done yet."

Rick followed him, shaking his head. "Where are you going?"

"To buy more gum." Mallard quickened his pace. "Something tells me I'm going to need it."

NO NEWS IS BAD NEWS

Three days passed, then four, and still there was no news of the amulet. The papers were having a field day with the story, grinding out editorials about the ineffectiveness of the police department. It was the same old story; when no new leads came up the press blamed the police, and when they blamed the police, Mallard's father — chief inspector — bore the brunt of it.

By the end of the fourth day, with no breaks, Mr. Westerman was like an angry bear, ready to lash out at the slightest provocation.

"I don't know if I could stand it around here," Rick said, sitting in Mallard's room that fourth night. They'd been listening to music — Mallard's way of forgetting his problems for a while — and Rick was talking between records. "It's like going around with a grenade in your hand all the time—just waiting for it to pop."

"Oh, it's not so bad. He's just having job trouble. It happens all the time," Mallard answered calmly.

The new record started, and they went back to listening. Two albums later, Rick left, and Mallard went to bed. He lay awake until midnight and then finally dozed off, only to awaken when he heard his father come in. It was about one in the morning, perhaps a bit later, and Mallard got up to greet him. With his mother away visiting her sister, Mallard tried to be around when his dad got home.

"Hi, Dad. Rough day?"

Mallard needn't have asked. His father looked like a cat that had been dragged through a knothole backwards.

"Yeah."

"No new leads?"

"None." Mr. Westerman sat down at the kitchen table and put his head in his hands. "Nothing — not even a smell. They haven't tried to sell it or move it. No man in a green suit has been seen. Nothing. It's like they'd vanished."

"Want some coffee?" Mallard stood and went to the sink. "It helps sometimes to get your mind off things."

"No. I'm coffeed out. I think I'll just try to catch some sleep. I have to be back at the office in about six hours." He rose and made his way to the bedroom; Mallard heard the springs squeak as he flopped down, clothes and all.

Mallard waited three or four minutes; then he went into the bedroom. Inspector Westerman was already sound asleep.

Mallard reached down and unlaced his father's shoes, took them off, then loosened his dad's belt and tie and covered him with a blanket. As he left the bedroom, he unplugged the bedside phone and carried it into his room, where he plugged it into the wall socket.

No sense in letting a ringing phone wake Dad, he thought, sliding under his own covers. He closed his eyes and was just going under when the phone rang.

"Yes?" He grabbed it on the first ring.

"Malcolm? How are ya, kid? This is Peterson, down at headquarters. Can I talk to your dad?"

"Is it important? I hate to wake him if it isn't." Mallard sat up in bed. "I mean he's really exhausted."

"Oh. Well, I guess not. It can wait until morning. Why don't you just leave him a note — tell him to call headquarters as soon as he gets up."

"What is it?"

"Probably nothing, really." Peterson's voice showed the strain. "It's just that with all the pressure any lead looks good. Somebody broke into the zoo and stole three nine-foot cobras."

"The curse," Mallard felt the hair on his neck rise, "on the back of the amulet."

"Yeah. That's what we figured, especially when we saw the note."

"What note?"

"Whoever took the cobras left a little note in the cobra cage."

"What did it say?" Mallard asked.

"Something about the lord of the underground — just a minute, I have a copy of it right here." Mallard heard paper being shuffled, then Peterson came back on the line. "Yeah, here it is. It says: 'Beware the curse of the lords of the underworld. Kofren lives

again and will exact vengeance.'"

"That's it?"

"Yeah. It's made out of headlines cut from the newspaper, glued on a notebook pad. We've already checked it for prints. There were none. The lab is going over it for other clues, and we've got half a dozen officers checking around down at the zoo. I guess there's nothing else we can do for now. But listen, Malcolm—make sure your dad knows I called, okay?"

"Yes, I'll leave a note. Don't worry," Mallard assured him. Peterson hung up; Mallard put the phone in the cradle and lay back, his eyes closed.

There was something about the note, something that Mallard could sense but couldn't quite bring into the open.

Lord of the underworld, he mused. It might not mean anything, but if it did? What if it meant that the person who stole the amulet, and then the cobras, was somehow linking himself to the ancient Egyptian underworld? Could *that* mean that he was actually living underground somewhere?

The idea was pretty crazy, a grab in the dark, really, but worth checking. Mallard re-

membered a newspaper story he'd seen about some old missile silos. There was one right outside of town, and a few more scattered around the county. Built in the late fifties, the silos had been sold at auction about a year before because they were obsolete. A local columnist had jumped on the story to make some scathing comments about defense spending.

Mallard got out of bed and hurriedly put on his clothes. It wasn't worth waking his dad to investigate a hunch this wild, not when the inspector needed sleep so badly. But it was something Mallard *had* to check, something his gut feelings made him do.

He finished tying his shoes and walked quietly down the hall. For a moment he thought of leaving a note, but he decided it would just worry his dad unnecessarily, especially if his hunch came to nothing.

Outside it was still pitch-dark. Mallard unlocked his ten-speed bike and started down the street.

He'd have to stop and pick up Rick, of course. That would take ten or fifteen minutes because he had to be careful not to awaken Rick's parents. They wouldn't understand.

Then it would take half an hour to hit the edge of the sleeping city, and another fifteen minutes or so to get to the silo area nearest town.

He shifted into fourth, then fifth, and increased the pump action in his legs. Mallard wanted to make the silo area before dawn, while it was still dark.

He'd have to hurry.

AN ILL-FATED HUNCH

"You're crazy. You're stark, raving bananas, that's what you are." Rick pedaled to keep up with Mallard. "I mean coming and waking a guy by throwing rocks against the window — and then *breaking* the window!"

"I guess I threw a little hard. But you wouldn't wake up." Mallard flashed him a smile. "If you didn't sleep so soundly," he let it hang.

"Sure. It's all my fault, right? I mean what am I going to tell my folks about the window? I can just see their faces when I tell them the reason it's broken is that you came by and pulled a Huck Finn stunt with a rock. And why?" Rick caught up. "I'll tell you why — so we can go look at an empty hole in the ground."

"Rick."

"You're crazy—I'll say it again. Your mind has tipped over or something."

"I *told* you it was just a wild hunch." Mallard turned his head away from the deserted night streets, faced his friend, and let his bike coast. "If you think it's so crazy why did you come?"

Rick smiled. "Would you believe it if I told you I'm afraid to stay home and face the music about the window?"

"No." Mallard shook his head and answered the smile. "Because I know your folks, and they wouldn't really be all that upset. Come on, the truth, now."

"All right," Rick sighed. "I'm with you because I've seen your hunches pay off when I didn't think they stood a chance."

"And you wouldn't want to miss anything, right?"

"Yeah." Rick nodded. "That's right."

"Okay, then, let's quit jabbering and ride."

The two were silent as they bicycled down the long stretch of Elm Street that led to the edge of the city—silent as the dead, predawn streets.

At the city limits Elm turned into County Road Nineteen, and they kept pedaling until

they were well away from the city. Only then did Mallard realize how dark it was. Without the overhead streetlights and signs, he could barely see his handlebars.

"How much farther?" Rick was panting.

"About three miles. Maybe a little more." Mallard, too, was having trouble catching his breath. "Another thirty minutes."

"Can't we slow down a little?"

"No, not yet. I want to be sure to get there while it's still dark. If this hunch pays off, we don't want to be caught in the daylight."

"Just between us, *I* don't want to be caught in the dark either," Rick snorted. "Maybe you're forgetting, but it's likely that whoever we're going up against has three nine-foot cobras on *his* side."

They came to a slight upgrade, and Rick shifted down. "As if it makes any difference how long they are."

Mallard slowed. In the darkness he'd almost passed the gravel road that led off through the woods to the missile silo area. "Here. We've got to turn here."

He swung off the pavement onto the gravel, and Rick followed. "How did you know? There isn't a sign or anything."

"I remember a map they had in the paper," Mallard answered. "I think it's about another mile from here to the silo."

It was rough going on the gravel because the tires on the bikes were so narrow. Even so, the two covered the mile in just over ten minutes. Mallard pulled his bike off the road into a ditch.

"Here?" Rick squinted and tried to peer through the darkness. "What's different about this spot?"

"This is where the silo is," Mallard said softly.

"I don't see anything."

"Of course not — it's underground. They were built so nothing would stick up in case of a nuclear blast. The silos are almost invulnerable." Mallard turned away. "Come on. If I'm right there should be a chain link fence just across the ditch — ahh, yes, here it is."

Mallard turned left and walked beside the fence until he came to a small gate. It was hanging open, the hinges rusted, and he slipped through.

"They used to have guard dogs patrolling the fences," he whispered to Rick, "when it was in operation."

"Yeah. Now they've got guard cobras."

"Oh, come on, don't be ridiculous. Let's go find the silo — I'm beginning to think I was wrong. That gate hasn't been moved in years."

Mallard led the way to a huge, round, concrete slab about forty feet across. It looked as though someone had made an immense, circular floor several feet thick and then forgotten to make walls or a roof.

"This is the lid. It's divided in the middle, see? In an emergency the two parts would open, and the missile would come up on an elevator."

"Clever," Rick remarked.

"Yeah," said Mallard. "In the center there's a big, hollow core, going down about a hundred feet. That held the missile, always ready to fire. Then, all around it and arranged in floors, were rooms and offices and storage places." Mallard moved around the slab until he came to a concrete buttress set in the ground so it leaned over like the old basement entryways on houses. In the middle there was a steel door, with a pulley and counterweights so it could be opened easily.

The door wasn't locked.

"After you," Rick said. "And I do mean *after* you."

Mallard tried the door; it opened with only a quiet squeak.

"Somebody has oiled the hinges," Mallard whispered.

"Probably the same guy who stole the necklace and cobras."

"Come on. Let's go in and see if there's anything down there." Mallard stepped carefully inside and found himself on a metal stairway. It was pitch-dark. He reached for his pocket flashlight and clicked it on.

"Oh, no," he muttered.

"What's wrong?" Rick's voice was hoarse with dread.

"The flashlight batteries are dead. I meant to change them last week. Nuts!"

Rick was too busy fighting for control of himself to manage a reply.

Mallard held still for a moment or two, sensed rather than saw Rick in back of him, then started down the steps, carefully feeling his way.

"I hate to say it, but I have this sinking feeling," Rick whispered weakly.

"Yeah—it is a little weird."

They followed the stairway down to a cement floor. Mallard reached out to his right and felt a wall. To his left there was nothing.

"The missile pit is on the left," he hissed to Rick. "Stay to the right."

He was going to say more — that they'd better hold hands to keep from being separated in the darkness — when he heard a brief scuffling sound behind him.

"Rick?" He turned and faced the spot where Rick should have been. "Rick, are you all right?"

There was no answer.

"Rick?"

But there was nothing; nothing but silence, darkness, and the sudden realization that he was alone — alone in a black pit that had swallowed his best friend.

BIG TROUBLE

"Rick?"

Twice more Mallard tried calling, but there was nothing — no sound but his own breathing.

He moved back against the wall and stood silently, holding his breath, listening.

Nothing happened.

For five seconds he stood that way, then another five. He was waiting, and he didn't know what he was waiting for — just that something would come from the dark, something that had taken his friend. Mallard wanted to be ready.

When it came it wasn't what he expected.

With barely a sound, strong hands suddenly pinned his arms to his side. Then something soft — cotton? — was placed over his mouth and nose. There was a horrible, pun-

gent smell; for a few seconds Mallard fought and kicked. Then he fell beneath a roaring red cloud that covered his brain like a forest fire.

He wasn't sure how long he was unconscious. It might have been a few minutes or a year; there was no way to tell.

But his eyes finally opened; there was light, and he found himself looking at a coarse cement floor.

"Mal?"

"Nnnhh?" Mallard tried to form a word, but his lips wouldn't move; his tongue seemed glued to the top of his mouth.

"Don't try to move. We're chained together," Rick warned. "I came out of it before you."

The back of Mallard's head felt as though it were being cut off with a dull saw. "It hurts," he managed to mumble. "My head."

"Yeah, I know. Just hang on and it will pass. I guess they used some kind of gas or ether on us. The pain only lasts for a few minutes."

Mallard nodded, winced, and lay still. He was chained back-to-back with Rick; the boys' wrists were tightly bound with some kind of chain. The links bit deeply into Mallard's

flesh, and he moved slowly to try to ease the pain.

"Where are we?" The pain in his head was beginning to lessen. It didn't hurt to talk.

"I have no idea," Rick answered. "From my side it looks like a cement room with a light bulb. What do you see?"

Mallard looked up. "A wall. About a foot away."

"That's it, then. We're in a small, square room with one light bulb and a door."

"We're also," Mallard said, sighing, "in trouble. I guess we've found the thief who stole the amulet and cobras."

"How about if we don't talk about the cobras?" Rick's voice was tight. "We've got enough to worry about without them."

"Yeah — I agree. What we have to do is figure a way to get out of this mess and get word to Dad."

"Well, *you're* the one with the brain. Go to it." Rick laughed drily. "But unless you've got a hacksaw, I don't see much future in thinking. These chains are tight, and I think they've used a padlock to keep them in position. I really can't see any way to get them off."

"*You have dared to invade the underworld*

of King Kofren!" The voice sounded like deep thunder; it was almost loud enough to break the boys' eardrums.

"What was that?" Rick had jumped with the sudden booming: The chains tightened.

"A loudspeaker, the way it sounded. It's probably right outside the door."

"*For this transgression you must suffer the test of all those who dare play with the gods!*"

"Oh, come *on!*" Mallard yelled. "This is ridiculous; you can't get away with it. Why don't you just let us go?"

"*Silence, mortal!*"

"Well, could you at least turn the volume down and come in here so we can see you?" Rick asked.

"*Mortals may not see the divine Kofren! Not until they have passed the test of the ages!*"

With that the voice went to silence, and for five minutes the boys lay, trussed like slaves on the way to ceremonial slaughter, waiting for something to happen.

When nothing did, Mallard twisted his neck so he could whisper to Rick. "Apparently he has a mike or something in here, so we'd better hold it down. I think we're dealing with a maniac."

"Yeah," Rick agreed. "Or a reincarnation of the real King Kofren. What do you think the test is supposed to be?"

"I'd rather not think about it, frankly," Mallard replied. "It probably isn't very pleasant."

"That's what I was thinking. As a matter of fact, I was thinking that any kind of test he dreams up will probably involve those snakes."

Rick stopped as the door, which moved sideways on sliding tracks, suddenly opened four inches.

Mallard was lying the other way and couldn't see, but could hear, the door. "What's happening?"

"The door opened," Rick answered. "Just a couple of inches. Other than that, nothing."

"Can't you see anything through the crack?"

"No," whispered Rick. "There's not much light out there. Wait! Something moved."

"What was it?"

"A hand. I think it was a hand with a gold bracelet. Now it's gone. But there's something at the opening, down on the floor."

"What?"

"I'm not sure, but it looks like a basket of

some kind, with a little sliding hatch on it."

Rick's body suddenly stiffened. Mallard heard his partner gasp.

"What is it?"

Rick hissed the answer, "The hatch opened."

"And?"

"There's a cobra coming into the room!" Rick's voice sounded like a guitar string stretched to the breaking point. "It was in the basket, and it's coming into the room."

"Which way is it heading?"

The answer came slowly, finally, like the blows from a deadly hammer, as the door slid shut.

"It's coming right at my *face*."

COBRA BAIT

"Lie still—absolutely still," Mallard whispered, forcing himself to relax. "I read somewhere that cobras only strike if threatened—if you make them angry. How close is it?"

"Two, three feet. Its head is raised."

Mallard could feel Rick's body shaking. "Relax—just keep *relaxed*."

"It's spreading its hood! It's going to strike!"

"Easy," Mallard made his voice smooth, slow. "Just stay quiet and calm. Don't move and don't talk."

He could feel Rick hold himself steady, fighting for control.

Darn, if I could only *see*, Mallard thought, see what is going on. But he was afraid to turn over, afraid that his movement would trigger the snake.

For a minute, then another, nothing happened. And when five full minutes had passed — Mallard forced himself to count — he decided to chance it.

"How is the snake now?"

"I don't know. I've got my eyes closed," Rick answered in a whisper. "Let me open them. Ahh, it's backed off—gone over to the corner."

"Well, keep your eye on it while I try to figure a way to get out of these chains. I've got a paperclip in my pocket, and if I can just scrabble around and get it out, maybe I can pick the padlock."

"Settle down!" Rick hissed the warning. "The snake is raising its head — it's getting upset!"

Mallard froze and waited. "Is it calm yet?"

"No — wait, yes, its head is going back down."

"All right, keep your eye on it."

"Don't worry. I couldn't look anywhere else."

Mallard went back to his search and finally, after bending his wrist almost backwards, he fished the paperclip out of his pocket. Working slowly he straightened the wire holding it in back of his waist—and felt for the padlock.

"How are you doing?" Rick asked.

"Shh—I'm just now finding the lock. Give me a minute. Unnh, just a bit more. There!"

"Did you get it loose?"

"No. I found the lock. Oh, good, it's just a simple little thing." His voice trailed off as he concentrated on getting the wire in the lock.

"How did you ever learn to pick locks?" Rick kept a wary eye on the snake, which had relaxed and coiled upon itself in the opposite corner. "A cop's kid like you learning to do something illegal?"

"Sometimes it is necessary to understand criminal methods to understand criminals," Mallard answered primly. "Besides, Dad brought home a police brochure that showed all about lock picking. Naturally, I studied it."

"Naturally."

"How's the snake?" Mallard asked.

"All right. I just hope it doesn't get hungry —you ought to see the size of it."

"Don't worry. They eat small rodents. It won't strike us unless we frighten or anger it."

"That's nice to know," Rick snorted. "When I get nailed, I'll at least know the reason."

"Easy — it's not going to attack us. Not

now, anyway, while it's settled down." Mallard had the wire in the lock and was working to get it angled through the small tumblers, clicking one at a time. "Just two or three more."

"Even if we get loose, the snake's in the corner by the door," Rick said. "I don't see how we can get past it."

"Well...that...is...something...we'll...have...to...work...on...when we come to it." Mallard strained to warp his wrist at the right angles. *There!* It's loose."

He quickly pulled the lock out of the chain and felt the tightness ease. In ten seconds he'd unwrapped their wrists and turned over —slowly—to face the snake. It was the first time he'd seen it.

"Lord—it's huge!"

The noise of the chains and Mallard's movement as he turned over aroused the reptile; it raised its head and spread its hood.

"Oh," Mallard whispered.

The head was a full four feet above the floor; it towered like an evil beacon of death, moving slowly back and forth.

"See?" Rick hissed. "I *told* you it was scary."

"All right, all right. I agree. But listen, it's

over in that corner, and cobras can only strike the distance they're raised up. Which means it can't even reach us from where it is."

Mallard stood suddenly, and the snake swung silently to follow the movement. It didn't strike.

"See? It's all right. Come on, stand up."

Rick got up slowly and stood next to Mallard.

The snake swiveled to cover Rick, then moved back to Mallard — back and forth, silently watching both boys.

"I wish I had a snake charmer's flute," Rick said. "Or, better yet, a snake charmer."

"Yeah—wait, that gives me an idea. We've got to get the thing away from the door, right?"

"Right. But...."

"So we'll do the same thing as a snake charmer. We'll give it something to look at, distract it, while we get the door open."

"Mal...."

"You go over to the opposite corner and move around. Keep its attention."

"I *knew* that was what you were going to say. Now I'm cobra bait, right?"

"Just go. And remember, it can only strike the distance it's raised off the floor. Stay

farther away and it can't reach you."

"That's easy for you to say."

"Go!"

"All right, all right." Rick got up, like frozen molasses, and moved slowly across the floor to the opposite corner.

The snake turned to watch him, then turned back to Mallard; when Mallard kept still, it looked back to Rick.

"*Move* a little. Keep it occupied," Mallard whispered without moving.

"You mean like a small rodent?"

"Rick!"

Rick shrugged, to ease the tension in his shoulders, and tried weaving back and forth. The cobra matched the weaving and slid forward to meet the new threat.

Mallard eased toward the door, a fraction of an inch at a time, until his hand rested on the metal handle. He pushed slowly.

The door wasn't locked! The person wearing the gold bracelet must have assumed that the snakes would take care of the two boys. The thought made Mallard shiver. He pushed against the door. It moved sideways, opened half a foot, and he pushed harder until it was open two feet.

The snake's attention was still riveted on

Rick, who was doing a jiggling dance. Twice the snake had flared to strike, and twice it had held back, knowing its victim was just out of range.

Mallard looked at Rick over the snake's head. He nodded silently and made a motion for Rick to come around the snake — which had glided away from the door.

Come on! Mallard's mind shouted the words but he was afraid to speak; come on *now!*

Rick didn't need any urging. He carefully worked around the snake, which turned with him like a robot, until the two boys were side by side at the door. Then Mallard grabbed him by the shirt, pulled him through the opening, and quickly shut the door.

They were free.

TO THE UNDERWORLD

Once out of the room the boys found themselves on a catwalk that circled the inside of the silo. It was daylight outside, but only a little light filtered in around the slab above them. It was enough so they could see the empty hole, huge and yawning, and make out other catwalks above and below them, one for each floor level.

"How do we get out?" Rick stopped beside Mallard, put a hand on the railing, and pulled it back, covered with rust. "How do we get up out of here?"

Mallard didn't answer. He was thinking that they should go for his father, run for help, but something held him back. Some feeling wouldn't let him run.

"Come *on*," Rick urged. "Let's get out of here."

"Hold it."

"*Hold* it? Are you crazy? There are two more cobras around here someplace—or have you forgotten?"

"No, I haven't forgotten. But there's something wrong here; something doesn't make any sense about all this," Mallard puzzled.

"What do you mean?"

"I mean whoever stuck that cobra in with us should be around somewhere."

"Yeah. I know. Let's run."

"But there's nobody here."

"And you're *complaining*? Come on, let's get the heck out of here."

"No. We're staying. We're going to find out what's going on." Mallard's voice was firm. "I didn't come this far to turn it all over to the police."

"Your father will kill you if we get killed." Rick realized how silly he sounded but let it stand. "I mean it's crazy to stay."

But Mallard was gone, down a staircase— made of the same rusted metal—that led to the lower levels.

"Well, I can't leave you alone." Rick fol-

lowed, keeping an eye cocked on the cobra room as he went past the door.

Down they went, three levels and more, until the light filtering down from the cracks around the slab made only a subtle change in the darkness. Finally Mallard stopped; it was as low as they could go. Beneath them water had seeped in and filled the bottom of the silo.

"See?" Rick pulled up beside him. "There isn't anything. Now can we go?"

Mallard shrugged. "Yeah, I guess so. I could have sworn that we'd find something. Wait. What's that?"

He pointed to the other side of the silo, to a door.

Rick looked. "There isn't anything."

"Yes. I saw a flicker of blue light. I *know* it."

He moved off around the walk, and Rick followed reluctantly. It took ten seconds to get to the door, and when they arrived it was closed tightly.

"See?" Rick repeated. "It's just like the rest of them—there's nothing."

"Let's open it." Mallard grabbed the handle. Like the rest, it opened sideways.

The sight that met their eyes was like a vision from a dream, like looking into the

long-dead and ancient past. The two boys stood, frozen, before it.

The room was narrow and fairly long; it looked as if it might once have been used for storing pipes. But it had been cleaned out and painted with Egyptian murals, like some tomb paintings Mallard had seen in a history book. In the center of the room — flanked by two torches that gave off blue flame — was a golden throne surrounded by lush carpets.

The throne was empty.

"Wow," Rick breathed. "I mean *wow* — have you ever seen anything like this?"

"Only in pictures." Mallard was stunned. "I never expected anything like this — not in a million years. It's like...."

He was going to say it was like getting into a time machine and going back to ancient Egypt, back to the old days of the pharaohs and tombs; he was going to say that and more. But before he could get it out, an iron hand grabbed his neck from behind.

"Enter, mortals!"

The voice was at his ear, and before Mallard could turn, both he and Rick were thrown headlong into the blue room. The door screeched shut behind them.

Mallard looked up from the floor — looked

and didn't believe what he saw. He closed his eyes, opened them, tried to say something, and couldn't formulate the words.

He didn't have to. Rick had looked up at the same time, had seen the same thing, and spoke for both of them.

"It's him—it's Kofren!"

A FATAL MISTAKE

In the blue light he towered over them, a king from the past — or that's how Mallard felt for a moment. Just for a second, half a second, he thought it *was* Kofren, back from the world of the dead.

The man standing above them was more than six feet tall, dressed in the ancient funeral garb of the pharaohs: a folded, golden headpiece with cobra insignia, the golden amulet around his bare neck and chest, gold bracelet, silver wrap-around skirt, and golden sandals.

He locked the door with a padlock and strode silently past the two boys. From a stand next to the throne he lifted the symbolic flail and shepherd's crook. Crossing his chest with these objects, he turned majestically and sat.

"It's *him!*" Rick said again. "It's the king."

"No." Mallard shook his head. "It's startling, I'll admit. But he's no pharaoh. I saw a white band on his wrist when he walked past. It must have been left by a watch. He's not a king, he's a maniac."

"*Silence, mortals!*" The voice thundered forth, and Mallard realized that the madman must have hidden a portable mike under the amulet — a mike that sent his voice booming through a central public address system. "*Silence in the presence of gods!*"

Mallard closed his mouth, made a sign to Rick to do the same, and waited.

"*You have trespassed on the inner regions of the underworld — for that you must die!*"

"Now wait a minute...." Rick started, but Mallard held a hand up to stop him.

"For this trespass we are truly sorry, O king of kings," Mallard walked forward and kneeled before the throne. "It was done in ignorance. Please forgive us."

"What?" Rick looked at him. "Are you crazy?" he whispered.

Mallard signaled Rick to follow his lead. Rick shrugged, came forward, kneeled, and mumbled an apology. If Mallard had gone nuts, Rick thought, he might as well follow.

"Apologies aren't enough! You must pay the penalty!"

Rick stared at the man's face. It was heavily made up, like the faces of the ancient Egyptian kings, and the eyes had a strange, tight look. "Why, he's nuttier than a fruitcake! He actually thinks he's Kofren."

"Shut up!" Mallard hissed. "Play along with him until we can...."

"Observe, mortals, what happens to transgressors!"

The phony king pushed a button on the arm of the throne, and the boys could hear a faint whirring sound. For a moment they could see nothing; then, at the other end of the room a sliding panel revealed a lighted cubicle covered with glass.

In the cubicle stood a fattish man in a green suit. His eyes were open and staring, but they couldn't see anything.

Down at his feet lay the two missing cobras.

"He's dead!" Rick's voice was hushed. "It's the man who stole the amulet, and he's dead."

"He wished to profit from the gods by selling the sacred amulet of the sun! For that he had to die. Just as you have to die, lest you

reveal the hidden underworld to other mortals!"

"We won't tell anyone, O king of kings." Mallard lowered his head between his hands. "We won't reveal your secret."

"*You lie!*"

Again the madman pushed a button on the armrest of the throne, and again there was a whirring sound. Mallard looked up but could see nothing out of the ordinary.

But Rick looked in a different place.

"The case," he said, his voice trembling, "where the body is — the glass is sliding away."

Mallard swung his head. Sure enough, the glass had moved away from the body in the cubicle, and even as he watched, one of the cobras slithered out onto the floor. The other followed.

Rick jumped up and made for the door, forgetting it was locked.

"*Running is useless, mortals. You cannot escape.*"

Mallard rose to his feet, one eye on the snakes. "They can bite you too," he cautioned.

"*They will not harm the gods!*"

"But you're not a god. Unlock the door,

now, so we can all get away from them," Mallard urged.

It was useless. The man on the throne was mad and would hear nothing but what he wanted to hear.

Mallard moved away from the throne, over to the door near Rick.

"Can you pick this lock? Like the other?" Rick whispered hopefully.

Mallard looked at it and shook his head. "No — It's a better lock — too complicated."

"Then we're stuck."

Mallard nodded. "Yeah. Looks that way. Our only hope is to keep away from them, try to get around them"

"I'm scared, Mallard."

"Yeah — me too. Look, Rick, I'm sorry about dragging you in."

Rick tried to force a reassuring smile but could only manage a grimace.

"Just so you know," Mallard finished.

"All right, I know."

For a moment they stood silently, watching the snakes. The cobras had come around, one on either side of the throne, and were gliding toward the door.

True to the madman's word, the snakes didn't pay any attention to him — probably

because he sat still. Instead they concentrated their attention on getting away. They seemed to know that the door led out, and that's the way they headed—straight for the boys.

"We've got to get around them, get back to the other end of the room," Mallard whispered, moving off to the right.

"But there's no room—it's too narrow."

"Yeah. But we've got to *try*. We can't just stand here and die without doing something," Mallard insisted. "Maybe we can get past them and jump the guy and get the key or something."

Mallard made a move, but it was already too late. As soon as he started forward, the snakes raised their heads and spread their hoods, weaving gently and slowly. The cobras were ready, and the way they were situated made it impossible to get around them—they covered the whole span of the narrow room.

"Well, that's that." Mallard looked at his friend. "Oh, lord, Rick...."

They were about to die, and they knew it, when the man on the throne made his first, and last, mistake. He stood, raised one huge arm, and pointed dramatically at the boys: "*And now die, mortals!*"

All snakes are sensitive to vibration—they cannot hear, but they "feel" sound — and when the loudspeaker thundered, it upset them. They turned and saw the sudden movement of the madman; the arm with its glistening gold bracelet was within easy range.

Both evil heads darted, both snakes struck as one and buried their fangs deep, so the poison went in solid. At that precise instant Mallard saw his chance.

"Come *on!*" He grabbed Rick, dragged him around the snakes—which were too occupied to bother with them—and raced to the safety of the other end of the room.

And then there was nothing to do but wait: wait until the poison took its deadly toll, wait until they could get the key to the door lock off the body and lure the snakes away.

Wait until they could get out and run, run up through the silo, to their bikes and the fresh light of day; wait until they could leave this evil place and *run*.

THE METHODS OF MADNESS

"His name was Anton Pullmer. Anton J. Pullmer." Mallard's father made no attempt to conceal his fatigue. "And he's been in and out of mental institutions for the past twenty years. He was a sick man."

They were back in the museum. It was the day after the boys had escaped from the silo. It had been a day of excitement and of tying up loose ends.

Inspector Westerman, of course, was in a frenzy by the time the boys returned. Mallard explained what had happened as calmly as he could and apologized for not having awakened his father when Peterson called. But, torn between relief for his son's safety and fury at what he considered Mallard's negligence and foolishness, it took a while for the chief to calm down. As soon as he did, he ordered a

task force back to the silo. They left at once, accompanied by a team of experts from the zoo.

"This has to be the strangest case I've ever seen." Mallard's father looked down at the amulet, which was back in the case. "When I went into that room...."

He let it die and shuddered, remembering the scene—the bodies, the strange blue light.

"It was sad—*is* sad," the chief remarked. "Pullmer was a brilliant and highly educated man — graduated from college when he was nineteen, with degrees in zoology and physics, and then won a fellowship to study history. He cracked up in graduate school, at about the same time that he inherited a great deal of money. The estate was managed for him until he was released from the last institution — apparently cured."

"What was wrong with him?" the museum director asked. "I mean clinically?"

"He was a schizoid—an acute case of schizophrenia, split personality. They thought they had him cured and released him. Then he got the money from his estate and bought the silo for ten thousand.

"Then his madness took over. He thought —no, according to the doctors he actually *became* Kofren, at least in his mind. So he turned the silo into an underworld and stole the amulet. Of course when he took the amulet he wasn't really stealing but just taking back something that belonged to him. Or so he thought. The same for the snakes; he took them because they were part of the whole Egyptian world he was building. But it wasn't really stealing. Cobras have always belonged to kings."

"What about the dead man in the cubicle?" Mallard asked.

The inspector shrugged. "He was named Slater — a local small-time crook who had been in and out of jail since he was a kid. Pullmer hired him for the one job, probably found him in some bar. Then when Slater tried to talk him into selling the amulet, Pullmer turned the snakes loose on him."

Mallard grimaced, remembering how Pullmer had died. "It's a terrible way to go," he said with a shiver.

"Don't think about it. Just let the memory fade." His father reached down and wrapped an arm around his shoulder. "Try to forget what happened."

"I'll try." Mallard forced a smile.

They walked away from the amulet, toward the door, and they'd almost crossed the gallery before Mallard realized that Rick wasn't following them. He was still standing next to the glass case, looking down at the amulet.

Mallard went back to him. "Come on — what's the matter?"

"What?" Rick looked up; he'd been so engrossed in the necklace he hadn't heard. "What did you say?"

"I said what's the matter?" Mallard smiled.

"Oh. Nothing, really. I was just looking at the amulet and thinking of something."

"What?"

"Well, it's probably silly. A coincidence or whatever, but I was just remembering what it said on the back of the amulet. The curse."

"Yeah." Mallard closed his eyes and recited from memory. "'Whosoever shall use the power of this amulet wrongly shall die of the cobra's sting.' So what?"

"So has it occurred to you that the curse came true? Pullmer used the power of the amulet wrongly and died of the cobra's sting — just like it said."

"Oh." Mallard looked down at the amulet, nestled on its velvet cushion; it looked peace-

ful and beautiful, not at all deadly. "Yeah—I guess it did work out that way, didn't it?"

"Yeah. It did, didn't it?"

"Come on, let's go."

Rick followed him, and they walked toward the door, where Mallard's father waited to take them home.

But just before they reached the door Mallard turned and looked back at the amulet. It was a parting glance, a quick shot, but a strange thing happened—something he never told his dad or even Rick.

Just as he turned back, a certain feeling came over him — a kind of relief from the ugliness he'd seen. It was like a spell, unreal yet real, and it left him feeling warm and pleasant. He would never tell anybody, never say a word about it.

But he could have sworn the amulet was thanking him.